GET READY FOR A DAZZLING ADVENTURE WITH
INDIANA JONES™

It is 1938. Dr. Roger Ballentyne has found what appears to be a map to the fabulous, long-lost treasure of the Queen of Sheba.

Dr. Ballentyne's latest project, a new diamond laser capable of cutting through the hardest materials in a fraction of a second, has attracted the attention of the Fascist forces occupying Ethiopia. They kidnap him in an attempt to possess the treasure and the laser.

You are George Ballentyne, the doctor's fourteen-year-old son. You will embark on an incredible journey to Ethiopia with Indiana Jones™, the world's greatest adventurer.

A forbidding desert, hostile natives, and the armed might of the Fascists await you.

If you make the *right* choices, you will save your father and find the treasure.

If you make the *wrong* choices, you, your father, and Indiana Jones™ will never be heard from again!

GOOD LUCK!

INDIANA JONES

and the
LOST TREASURE OF SHEBA

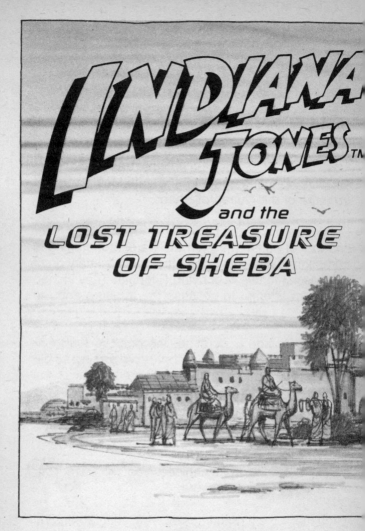

by **ROSE ESTES**
Illustrated by DAVID B. MATTINGLY

BALLANTINE BOOKS • NEW YORK

RLI: $\dfrac{\text{VL: } 5 + \text{up}}{\text{IL: } 5 + \text{up}}$

Library of Congress Catalog Card Number: 84-90850

ISBN 0-345-31664-9

Designed by Gene Siegel

Cover and interior art by David B. Mattingly

Manufactured in the United States of America

First Edition: June 1984

For Tom, best friend and colleague
—R. E.

INDIANA JONES™

and the
LOST TREASURE
OF SHEBA

Find Your Fate™ Adventure #2

It was ten thirty on a windy fall evening. I was nodding over my Italian lesson when suddenly I heard my father cry out in pain. I threw my bathrobe on and hurried into the hall. My hand was on the doorknob to my father's room when I heard a heavily accented voice say, "I want those blueprints, Doctor. Your laser is essential to us. We will do whatever is necessary to obtain them. If you refuse to help us, the consequences for you—and your family—will be serious. Melke, fetch the boy!"

I snatched my hand back and ducked into the hall closet just as the door opened. A tall slender man with blue tattoos on his face entered the hall. He moved in my direction and his heavily lidded gold eyes seemed to look straight at me. My heart was pounding so hard I was sure he would hear, but he only turned and crept silently toward my room.

My absence would be discovered within seconds. If I was to get help, I had to leave—and fast! Gathering my courage, I darted into the study, grabbed the pouch with the top-secret laser blueprints, and slipped out the front door. Behind me there was an angry yell!

I ran for the elevator, dashed in, and punched the lobby button. The apartment door flew open and the man with the tattooed face rushed into the hall. For one long second we stared at each other—and then the elevator doors slid shut.

I rushed out of the elevator the second the doors opened and crashed into a man who stood in my path.

"Why don't you look where you're going?" he growled. His darkly tanned face looked oddly familiar, and after a hasty apology I asked, "Aren't you an archeologist? Isn't your name Missouri or Mississippi or something like that?"

The man examined me with bright blue eyes. "Close, kid. The name is Indiana Jones. But I don't know you."

"George Ballentyne," I said. "Dr. Roger Ballentyne is my father and he's in danger." Then I tried to explain what was happening upstairs.

"Doesn't sound good," growled Jones. "I'll go upstairs, you find a cop."

"But, Mr. Jones, they're dangerous!"

"Don't worry about me, kid. I'll be just fine." And he strode into the elevator.

Clutching the pouch tightly, I hurried out into the street. It took me several minutes to find a policeman and even longer to persuade him to follow me.

As the elevator doors opened on our floor

my fears were realized. The door to our apartment stood wide open!

I ran through the apartment calling my father's name. There was no answer except for a low moan of pain. And there, sprawled on the floor, was Indiana Jones!

Later, after the police had finished filling out their forms, Jones and I sat at the dining room table.

"I told you they were dangerous," I said.

"Okay, kid, so I made a little mistake," said Jones as he helped himself to my father's Scotch. "If I had waited for the cops, they would have gotten away. This way I got a good look at them. And they didn't get the blueprints or the map."

"Map! You know about the map?"

"Sure. Why did you think I was here?" Jones pulled an oilskin pouch out of his stained leather jacket. Then, scraping everything off the table, he opened the map and spread it wide.

"Ethiopia! The kingdom of Sheba!" he said, stabbing its yellowed surface with a tanned finger. "You know about your father's interest in archeology. Well, he found this map a year ago and I've been studying it. It's authentic, all right.

"Unfortunately, your father lives in his own little dream world, like most scientists. I could hardly believe it when I read this month's *Scientific Journal*. Do you realize he wrote about his work on the new diamond laser *and* the treasure of Sheba all in the same article?

"That's like putting an ad in the Sunday paper saying 'Come kidnap me!' Doesn't he have

4

any idea what's happening in the world? Ethiopia's been overrun by Fascists, and they're desperate for anything that will help their war effort—like your father's laser. And if they can find the treasure of Sheba, so much the better. They'll have all the diamonds they need for the laser, and they'll fill their war chests too."

"Why are we just sitting here?" I cried. "We've got to go after them!"

Jones sighed. "It isn't that simple, kid. Things are very dicey over there. You can't just waltz in and say please give me back my father and forget you ever heard about the treasure of Sheba."

"Well, what are we going to do?"

"*We*? *We* aren't going to do anything. *You* stay here. *I* go to Ethiopia."

"You're not going without me."

"Don't be stupid," Jones said. "What would I do with a kid? You'd be nothing but trouble."

I tried to speak calmly. "Mr. Jones, do you speak Italian?"

"Well, no. But I speak pidgin African."

"I speak Italian, Mr. Jones. My father and I have studied it for the last year. I have also studied Ethiopia. And," I said quietly, "the man who has been kidnapped *is* my father."

"But you're just a kid!"

"I'm not a kid. I'm fourteen years old and at the top of my class. I'm in excellent physical condition and have earned sixteen Boy Scout merit badges as well as my marksman's medal."

"Boy Scout badges?" groaned Jones. Then,

before I could reply, he held up his palm and said, "Okay! You win. But the first time you complain, I send you home."

"I shall not complain, sir."

"That's what I'm afraid of," muttered Jones. "Okay, let's look at our choices."

Bending over the fragile map, I pointed to two areas that were circled in red.

....

1. *"If they're looking for the treasure, they might have taken him to Lalibela. It's an ancient site, and I know my father thinks that's where the treasure is hidden." Turn to page 71.*

2. *"I disagree. I think there's more of a chance that they took him to Addis Ababa," said Jones, pointing to the second circle on the map. "That's where the Fascists' headquarters in Ethiopia are." Go on to page 7.*

As our freighter approached the Red Sea port of Djibouti, Jones turned to me and said, "George, have you had the feeling that someone's been watching us these last few weeks?"

"That fellow with the squint seems to hang around a lot."

"Yeah, I thought so too."

As the rusty prow of the boat slid through the sapphire water and the dock drew closer, I glanced around nervously. "What should we do?"

"Ignore him. Maybe he'll go away once we dock."

But when the ship thumped against the massive wooden dock and porters swarmed aboard, the man with the squint continued to hover nearby.

Brushing the porters aside, Jones picked up our luggage and headed down the swaying gangplank.

"Welcome to Africa," he said as the strong smell of donkeys, camels, and people assailed my nostrils and swarms of flies buzzed around my head. Without the sea breeze the heat pounded down relentlessly. As we pushed our way through the crowd, my vision began to blur and I felt my knees go weak.

"Hey, kid, don't faint on me! There's some shade near that building. Can you make it?"

Somehow I got there and collapsed in the meager shade.

"Here, suck on this salt tablet," said Jones.

"It's the heat. It affects everyone at first. You get used to it after a while."

Slowly I opened my eyes and saw two figures before me. I shook my head to clear it and realized that one of the figures was our squinty companion from the ship. I opened my mouth to shout a warning, but I was too late. He slammed a stick down on Jones's head and Jones staggered and nearly fell. Turning, Jones wrenched the stick out of the man's hand and began to beat him with his own weapon.

At the first blow the man began to screech—

9

high, shrill cries that soon attracted a crowd of natives. Responding to the man's cries, they fell upon Jones and dragged him into a larger square. The squinty man danced alongside, clutching his head and howling loudly.

Alarmed, I hurried after them.

The crowd turned in at an imposing pair of gates, filed into a huge courtyard, and stood facing a large stone-and-adobe house. After a moment the wooden doors opened and out stepped an old, old man dressed entirely in white.

The squinty man hurried forward.

Pointing the index fingers of both hands at Jones, he began to wail and shout accusingly. After listening for a time, the old man held up his hand for silence.

Turning to Jones, who struggled in the grip of two muscular men, he spoke in an unfamiliar language.

"I'm an American!" shouted Jones. "Call off your goons!"

"Ah! I speak American," said the old man. "Unfortunately, my deputies cannot release you. You have been charged with a serious crime— striking a citizen without cause. Our country is ruled by stern laws. Should you be found guilty, your hand will be struck off by the sword."

"What if I'm judged innocent?"

"Then you will be released."

"And where does this all happen?" asked Jones. "I don't see any halls of justice."

"Our ways are different, sir. This is your

hall of justice," said the old man, waving toward the courtyard. Pointing to the crowd, who followed his every motion, he said, "They are the witnesses. I am the judge."

....

1. *"I don't like this setup, kid,"* Jones said out of the corner of his mouth. *"When I give the signal, run!"* Turn to page 12.

2. *"We'd never make it,"* I whispered. *"Stay and take your chances. This fellow looks honest."* Turn to page 13.

"Run, kid!" bellowed Jones. Then he shed the two guards who held him, grabbed my arm, and we fled as though the very devil were chasing us. Up and down narrow streets we ran, with the crowd howling in pursuit. No matter which way we dodged, they were always there, drawing closer. More and more people joined them at every turn until it seemed that the entire town was on our heels.

I tried to keep up, but soon my vision began to blur and my legs went rubbery.

"Don't do this to me, kid!" cried Jones. But I couldn't help it.

"You go on without me. I'll try to stall them," I gasped as I sank to the ground.

"Don't be dumb, kid. That's not my style." And putting his fists up, Jones turned to face the crowd.

THE END.

Jones reluctantly agreed. Then, turning to the old man, I said, "I have read of your open-air courts and believe that an innocent man can clear himself. We have no objection to being judged, because Mr. Jones is innocent."

"Well spoken, young man," said the judge. "If the defendant will promise good behavior, my deputies will release him."

"Give him your word, Jones," I whispered.

Jones growled and then said, "I promise. I've got nothing to hide."

And at a gesture from the old man, the deputies released Jones.

The next few hours were very interesting. The squinty man, whose name was Fantu Sharif, insisted that Jones had attacked him without provocation. Jones denied the charge, and the crowd joined in with their own comments. Finally the judge spoke.

"It is my opinion that Mr. Sharif has not proved his charge. Therefore, it is my decision that the matter be dropped. Mr. Sharif, you will pay the court costs and let this be the end!"

Fantu Sharif paid the deputies and slunk off with a glare of murderous rage.

Turning to us, the judge said, "If you would care to join me, I would be pleased to have you as my guests for dinner. It has been a long time since I have had the chance to speak American."

Jones shook his hand warmly and said, "We'll be there!"

The judge, whose name was Ras Cabada, greeted us later that night and welcomed us to his home. He clapped his hands and a line of women filed through the room and placed baskets of food on a long, low table.

"Sit down, please," urged our host, and folding our legs beneath us, we seated ourselves on the Persian carpets that covered the floor.

"Eat!" said the ras, dipping his hand into a steaming basket.

Many baskets passed through the room that night, and long before the dinner ended I was struggling to stay awake.

Finally the meal ended with sweet seed cakes and syrupy wine, and Ras Cabada asked what had brought us to his country.

"Call it a whim," said Jones.

"This is a dangerous time and place for whims," said the ras. "Our country is no longer our own. The Fascists have gained control of it. A state of war exists. The wise man does not place himself in such danger for a whim."

"I'm also stubborn," Jones said, drawing on a thin, black cigar.

"What are your plans, if I may ask?"

"We're going to Addis Ababa, but I haven't decided how. We'll either buy some camels and strike off across the desert, or take the morning train."

"Whichever way you go, beware," warned Ras Cabada.

They talked for hours, and before long I fell asleep. Much, much later Jones helped me to my feet and we paid our final respects. Then we stepped out into the street. High above us, unfamiliar stars glittered in a black velvet sky.

"Well, kid, how should we get to Addis Ababa?" asked Jones.

....

1. *"We can catch the train and ride in comfort." Turn to page 16.*

2. *"Or we can hire some camels and rough it." Turn to page 44.*

It was early the next morning when Jones and I boarded the ancient train.

"There are a lot of Fascist soldiers," I whispered. "Are we in any danger?"

"Not really," Jones answered quietly. "Just avoid confrontations and we'll be okay."

Finally the train began to move.

"Why are we going so slowly?" I asked.

"This train, he only goes fourteen miles in one hour," said a man behind me. "He cannot go faster. That is why he takes three days to get to Addis Ababa."

"Three days? It's only five hundred miles away!"

"But the train, he stops every night for peoples to cook foods and for bandits."

"Bandits!" exclaimed Jones.

"Oh, yes. Shiftas—terrible bandits. If the train he goes at night, bandits can take a piece of his track and then the train he falls off and bandits kill us and steal all our monies."

At that moment two tall, dark-skinned men dressed in tribal robes approached us.

"Our seats," said one, prodding Jones with the butt of his spear. "You leave."

I thought Jones would refuse, but caution prevailed. "Don't mind if I do," he said. "The seat's too small for me anyhow."

We edged past the two men, but they made no move to take our seats.

"This red face is no warrior," jeered the second man as he jabbed Jones in the chest. "He is an old woman and needs to sit down." Then he sank the butt of his spear into Jones's stomach.

Jones doubled over, clutching his stomach and gasping.

"I do not wish to ride with this old woman," said the first man. Pinching Jones's neck in a paralyzing grip, he pulled him from his seat.

Jones fumbled for his whip, but his fingers lacked the strength to free it. His face was white with pain. The warrior walked Jones down the narrow aisle toward the open door.

"I shall toss this old woman off the train," he said. "She should not take up space reserved for warriors."

Trying not to panic, I looked around for help, but other than the soldiers, who seemed amused, everyone avoided my eyes. I knew I had to do something fast. I could:

....

1. *Fling myself on the warriors and try to free Jones. Turn to page 23.*

2. *Speak to the soldiers in their own language and try to persuade them to help. Turn to page 26.*

17

"Terrific! Here we are in the middle of the desert, miles from anywhere! We'll never get to Addis Ababa!" I muttered.

"Have faith," said Jones as he crawled to his feet. "I've been in worse spots than this. Trust me, everything will be fine."

And it was. Jones was a master of the whip, and by evening a rabbit and four small birds were roasting over our tiny fire.

The sun rose fast the next day, and soon the heat was unbearable. Though Jones spotted some hills in the distance at midday, it was evening before we reached them.

"You stay here, kid," he said. "I'm going to see if I can find some water."

I was too tired to speak. Sinking to the ground, I quickly fell into an exhausted sleep.

Much later I heard footsteps and something touched my side. I opened my eyes and saw a pair of polished boots!

As I scrambled to my feet, the officer turned and said in Italian, "Here's another of them!" And down the hill came Jones, followed by a group of soldiers whose rifles were all pointed at him.

"Well, I found out what was on the other side of the hill," Jones said with a crooked grin. "Can you make out what they're saying, kid?"

They were arguing about what to do with us. For a while it seemed they might just let us go. But in the end the officer, who kept staring at Jones, decided to take us to their camp in Addis Ababa.

"See, I told you we'd get there, didn't I?" said Jones.

"Yes, but I didn't expect it would be as a prisoner of the Fascists!" I answered.

"Keep it down, kid. We'll figure a way out of this."

We were loaded into a large canvas-covered truck and made to sit with our backs against the cab.

The officer riding up front didn't know it, but I could hear everything he said.

"I know that man's face. I can't place him, but it will come to me," he told his driver. "Stop at the orphanage and we will get rid of the boy. He is of no use to us. Then we'll take the man to headquarters and interrogate him."

When I told Jones, he tilted his hat over his eyes, smiled, and said, "Relax, kid. You worry too much." Then he went to sleep!

Two days later we reached Addis Ababa— a bewildering sprawl of stone, mud, and adobe buildings. Throngs of soldiers and white-robed natives crowded the streets. Camels, donkeys, horses, and children were everywhere. And there, rising up out of the center of town, was an ancient stone obelisk.

"My God!" gasped Jones. "If that's not what we're looking for, I'm a five-footed duck! The treasure's got to be under there somewhere!" He scrambled up for a better look, but a soldier forced him back into his seat.

The truck screeched to a halt and rough hands pulled me out. One of the soldiers, looking

19

bored and annoyed, shoved me through the door of a rundown church.

"I have a new charge for you, Father Prello," said the soldier as a fat monk in a rumpled cassock came forward. He pushed me into the monk's hands, then turned and walked back out the door.

"Just what we need, another mouth to feed," said the monk with a sigh.

"You don't have to feed me," I said in Italian. "I was afraid to tell them, but I was just exploring. My mother will be very angry if she finds out I was brought in. Please let me go. I won't do it again."

The monk looked at me closely and then smiled. Placing an arm around my shoulders, he walked me to the door. "Time is so short, young man. Let us pray that when you grow up, you are still exploring instead of soldiering. Go home now!"

I ran out the door just as the truck pulled away. I crawled up into the spare tire carrier and held on for dear life as the truck drove down the rocky street.

Just as I was beginning to wonder if I could hang on any longer, the truck pulled up in front of a large adobe building marked Military Headquarters. The tailgate was lowered, hiding me from view, and I could hear Jones cursing as they shoved him into the building.

My mind raced. What would they do to him? Would the officer remember where he had seen Jones before? Somehow I had to get him out of there. But how?

....

1. I could create some sort of diversion right away in hopes of freeing him. Turn to page 27.

2. Or I could wait for night and try to free him then. Turn to page 28.

Getting someone to help would take too much time. If anyone was going to rescue Jones, it would have to be me.

I moved up behind a warrior and hooked my foot around his just as he was about to take a step. Staggering off balance, he crashed into his companion, who lost his hold on Jones for one short moment. That was all Jones needed. He whirled, pulled his whip out, and slashed it down in a vicious arc. Unfortunately, it caught on a luggage rack.

Undaunted, Jones flung himself at the warrior and punched him in the face. The war-

rior tried to use his spear, but it jammed under a seat.

The second warrior got to his feet and, scrambling over a row of seats, approached Jones from the rear. I quickly followed him by wriggling under the seats. I pulled the bullwhip free and looped it around the man's neck, preventing him from spearing Jones.

Struggling wildly, the four of us fought and stumbled the length of the car as passengers fled before us.

Quite suddenly I realized that there was nowhere left to go. I stood in the doorway of the train watching the smooth white sand speed past. With a sneer the warrior reached up, unwound the whip from his neck, and pushed me out the door.

Sand is not soft, especially when you strike it at fourteen miles per hour. I tumbled to a halt and lay dazed and groaning on the ground. A moment later I saw Jones suffer the same fate.

I walked over to him slowly. Together we watched as the train puffed its way across the horizon and disappeared.

....

Turn to page 18.

"Please help my friend or he will surely be killed!" I cried in Italian.

"Why should we help?" asked a large soldier who lazed comfortably in his seat. "We don't even know you."

"Because he's rich and will reward you!"

Some silent agreement passed between the soldiers and they swarmed out of their seats and joined the fight. In a moment the aisle was filled with surging bodies. Then there was a roar of victory and the two natives were gone.

Whooping victoriously, Jones and several soldiers swaggered down the aisle.

"Where are they?" I asked worriedly.

"We persuaded them that walking was healthier!" answered one of the soldiers.

"I don't know what you said, kid," gasped Jones, "but it sure worked."

"I said you would reward them."

"Aha!" said Jones. He rummaged in his duffel and pulled out a bottle of whiskey. "I was saving it for an emergency. I think this qualifies."

The rest of the trip was spent in song and companionship.

After bidding the soldiers a warm farewell at Addis Ababa, we entered a market outside the walls. Then we purchased a pair of camels and dressed ourselves in native robes.

. . . .

Turn to page 44.

Watching the soldiers as they walked past my hiding place, I realized they had left the truck unguarded—with the motor on!

I slipped out from underneath the truck and slid into the driver's seat. I had never really driven before, but I knew I had to try. I moved the clutch and turned the wheel. There was a grinding shriek and the truck lurched forward, picking up speed with every passing second.

Startled faces flashed by, and I saw that I was heading straight for Jones and his captors!

Throwing up their hands, they broke away from Jones and ran, two seconds before the truck rammed into the building.

My head was spinning and the truck was spluttering when Jones wrenched the door open and flung himself in beside me.

"You learn this in Boy Scouts?" he asked, backing the truck free of the building and gunning it down the street.

"It just seemed like the right thing to do. Are we going to make it, Jones?" I asked as a flood of army vehicles took up the chase.

"I don't know, kid. Just hang on to your seat and pray!"

THE END.

While I was trying to figure out what to do, the truck was driven into a walled compound behind the building. Seconds later the driver climbed out and walked away.

It wasn't comfortable, but it seemed safe, so I stayed where I was until dark.

When night fell, I crawled from the rack, crouched behind a tire, and looked around. The main building was about twenty feet away. Made of adobe, it was windowless and topped by a corrugated iron roof resting on thick beams. Light shone through the space between the walls and the roof, and as I approached I could hear the murmur of voices.

There was no way I could climb that wall, but parked next to it was another of the large canvas-covered trucks. Keeping to the shadows, I crept over to it and climbed on top of it. From there it was easy to pull myself up onto the iron roof.

Directly beneath me several men were talking in Italian.

"What's for dinner, Nicco?" asked one.

"Same old thing, that cursed stew," replied the second.

"The professor seems to like it," said a third, and my heart lurched.

"Do you think he'll tell the commandant what he wants to know?"

"No. He's too stubborn. But if he doesn't, the commandant might kill him. You know how angry he gets."

I almost lost my grip but braced my foot

against a metal rib just in time. With my heart thumping, I crept along the edge of the roof, looking into each room as I passed. I found Jones quickly. He lay crumpled on a narrow wooden bed in a small, empty room lit by one bare bulb that dangled from the ceiling.

"Jones!" I whispered. "Up here."

"You've got to help me out of here, kid," Jones said when he saw me. "I met that officer at a top-secret meeting in London a couple of years ago. He hasn't remembered me yet, but when he does, he'll realize I'm not here on a holiday. Your dad's a few doors down. If I can get out, maybe we can spring him."

"Tell me what to do," I said.

Jones looked around the empty room. "There's not a lot to work with," he muttered. Then, staring up at the ceiling, he said, "I've got it. Look, kid, see the electric cord? The one that goes to the light bulb?"

"Sure," I said, looking at the thin wire that snaked over the roof beams. "But what good will that do?"

"See if you can reach it, then break it and drop it down to me."

"But, Jones," I argued, "you'll get electrocuted."

"I'll get killed if I stay here, kid. Just do as I say!"

Holding on to the edge of the roof, I reached out as far as I could and caught the cord with my fingertips. I pulled it to me, wrapped it around my hand, and yanked hard. Nothing happened. I tightened my grip and pulled as hard as I could. There was a popping noise and all the lights went out.

"Good boy," whispered Jones. "Now drop it down to me."

I did as he said, and seconds later his face appeared under the edge of the roof.

"I knew I should have gone on a diet," he grunted as he strained to pull his body through the narrow opening. Fortunately, the metal roof was old and rusty and Jones was able to force his way through.

Beneath us, men shouted and cursed in the darkness.

"Hurry," Jones said, running along the edge of the roof. "We've got to get your father out before the lights come back on."

I moved as quickly as I could, and soon we dropped onto the roof of the truck.

"Never tried to do this in the dark," mumbled Jones as he fumbled under the dashboard. But seconds later the enormous vehicle rumbled to life and Jones swung it around and pointed it at the building.

"Seems to me your dad should be right about there," he said as he gunned the motor. "Get down on the floor, kid. It's Humpty Dumpty time." As he let out the clutch the huge truck thundered straight toward the wall.

"But, Jones," I yelled in disbelief, "what if my father is next to the wall?"

"Pray, kid. Pray," said Jones and then we hit. Huge chunks of adobe wall and sheets of metal roofing crashed down on the hood of the truck.

Jones turned on the headlights. There, standing dazed in their glare, was my father!

Jones leaped out, grabbed my father, and dragged him into the truck.

Switching the lights off, he reversed the truck, floored the gas pedal, and screeched out of the compound.

"Jones?" asked my father shakily. "What are you doing here?"

"We came after you, Dad."

"George!" my father said, noticing me for the first time. "You shouldn't be here. It's too dangerous!"

"We'll argue about that later," Jones said through clenched teeth as the truck hurtled through dark and deserted streets. "Right now we have to stay alive long enough to get out of this country."

"No," said my father. "I'm not leaving yet. I've found the treasure."

"Are you crazy?" shouted Jones. "In about two seconds this town is going to be swarming with Fascists. And if they find us, we've had it! We've got to keep going!"

....

1. *"Roger, this is not a wise decision. We should leave." Go on to page 33.*

2. *"Jones, we've got to try to find the treasure." Turn to page 34.*

"I know how you feel, Roger," said Jones. "This hasn't been easy on any of us, and it's hard to leave now that we're this close. But the treasure has kept for 3,000 years. It'll keep for a few more."

"I guess you're right," my father said sadly. From that moment on we traveled in silence. Somehow Jones managed to avoid the patrols, and by morning we were well on our way to the coast.

The truck ran out of gas just as we reached the desert, and Jones drove it into a deep ravine. "Wait here, I'll be back," he said. Then he disappeared into the brush. Hours later he reappeared, followed by a small band of robed men. The men examined the truck inside and out, then hunkered down next to Jones and bargained.

An hour later, swathed in native robes, we rode into the desert on three rangy camels. My father turned and watched the high plateau slowly disappear behind us. "One day," he said softly, "one day, we'll come back."

THE END.

"We've got to get to the tunnels under the obelisk," said my father. "Addis Ababa is going to be sealed off in minutes. We'll never get out alive. Our only hope is to get rid of the truck and go underground. It's the last place they'd think to look—they'll never find us there."

Lights and sirens split the night air and finally Jones drove the truck into a dark alley and shut off the engine.

"We'll do it your way, Roger, but I hope you know what you're talking about."

My father grinned. "They brought me down into the tunnels, hoping I'd find the treasure for them. I lied. I told them I hadn't found it, but I have."

Creeping from shadow to shadow, we approached the obelisk in the center of the city. My dad pressed a carving high above our heads and a stone panel slid aside. We entered, and it slid shut behind us.

Total darkness pressed in on all sides and a musty, dry smell filled my nose.

A light flared and my father stood outlined in the glow of a torch. He handed it to Jones, lit another for himself, and then led the way down a dark corridor.

The path sloped at a steep angle. Ancient hieroglyphics covered the walls.

"What do these things say?" I asked.

"It's just the usual stuff, kid," said Jones. "You know, 'Death to all who enter.'"

A chill ran through me. "Aren't you worried?"

"No, you get used to it. But there's usually at least one nasty trap to take care of unwelcome visitors. Have you found it, Roger?"

"Yes, it's around this next corner. I haven't disarmed it. It still works."

At that moment a gust of air blew through the corridor, and the torches flickered.

Jones stopped and turned in a crouch. "Someone just opened the panel," he whispered. "Is there another way out?"

"The only other path is one I haven't explored yet. I'm not sure it's safe. There are a lot of stones loose in the ceiling."

"Why isn't anything ever simple?" groaned Jones. Then he said, "Well, I guess these are our choices:

....

1. *"We can take the known route, spring the trap on whoever is following us, and then grab the treasure and run." Turn to page 36.*

2. *"Or we can make it seem as though we went down the other corridor, take the unknown path, and hope for the best." Turn to page 41.*

35

"Do you think they know about this trap?" Jones asked my father as we crept down the known corridor.

"No, I never let them come this far. I told them it was dangerous and they weren't anxious to follow. Ahh, here it is."

Holding his torch high, my father pointed at the ceiling. "See those three large blocks? Well, the floor under them is pressure-sensitive. If you step under the first or third block, down they come."

"Dad, they're getting closer," I said as I caught the sound of voices behind me.

"We have to let them get close or they won't follow us," said Jones. "I'll go first, Roger. Then George, then you." Backing up, he got a running start, jumped onto the safe middle section, leaped the third square, and stood on the other side.

"Can you do it, George?" asked my father.

I was scared, but I just smiled and, imitating Jones, took a running leap.

I made the center square, but from there I didn't have room for a running start. How could I make it over the third square?

"Hurry, George," urged my father. But the more I stared at the square and the block, the more uncertain I became.

Then Jones was at my side. "Put your arm around my waist and do everything I do," he said, putting his own muscular arm around me. Backing up as far as possible, we ran together, matching stride for stride. And then we were over!

36

Seconds later my father stood beside us.

Before we could catch our breath, four soldiers carrying torches came into view.

"Come on!" cried Jones, and the three of us ran. As we turned a sharp corner I heard a deep groaning rumble, terrified screams, and then silence. I stopped, but my father urged me on.

"There's nothing we can do for them, George. Just remember, they would have killed us if they'd caught us."

It seemed to me that we walked for hours down dark and twisting corridors. Twice more we found and avoided traps that had been left by the ancient builders. Finally we stopped before a blank wall.

"Here it is," said my father. Pressing a set of stones, he opened another stone panel.

Then our torches were mirrored in a million gleaming surfaces. We were in a vast, splendid storehouse of treasure.

"So she wasn't just a myth," said Jones, shining his torch on casks overflowing with precious gems.

"No, she wasn't," my father said softly. Moving ahead, he began to climb a set of steps that ran through the center of the room. "Come, I want you to meet the Queen of Sheba."

The steps rose steeply and ended in a platform covered with tiles of gold.

A spectacular gem-studded throne stood in the center of the platform. But even more astonishing was the figure that sat on the throne. For a moment I thought she was alive, so real

did she seem. Then I realized that the figure sitting so regally on her throne had been gilded and then painted to appear alive.

"Imagine it, Jones," my father whispered in awe. "She's sat here for centuries guarding her treasure. Have you ever seen anything like it?"

"Never," said Jones. "You've made the find of a lifetime, Roger."

"*We've* made the find of a lifetime," answered my father. "If it hadn't been for you, none of us would be alive to see it. Now all we have to do is pick out a few small pieces to prove our story and get back to New York in one piece."

"I think we can manage that," said Jones with a grin. "I'm beginning to dislike those Fascists. And I have a feeling they won't win this war. One of these days it'll be safe to come back. And this will be waiting for us when we do."

"I'm coming too," I said. "Don't forget me!"

THE END.

"Hurry, Jones, I can hear them coming!"

"We've got to bait the trap," Jones said. He took off his hat and tossed it over to the spot my father pointed to.

"They'll trigger the trap if they try to pick it up," my father said grimly. "And we'll be free of them."

Then, turning off to our left, we headed down a second, much narrower corridor.

"Roger, I don't like the looks of that ceiling," whispered Jones, looking up. Immense boulders and large stones hung over us. And even as I watched they moved. Dirt and stones began to shower down on our heads.

"Let's get out of here," Jones whispered. The three of us raced down the corridor. We had scarcely gone twenty yards when terrified screams ripped through the air, followed by a loud rumbling and a great thump. There was a burst of air and both of the torches blew out. Then the earth heaved beneath out feet, the ceiling groaned and gave way, and the air turned thick with dust. Stones pelted us from above. I dropped to the ground, holding my hands over my head.

At last it stopped, and I heard Jones and my father calling my name. "I'm here," I said, and a torch flared. I was buried up to my waist in dirt and stones. Behind me, back the way we had come, the passage was blocked with stones and rubble.

"We'll never be able to go back that way," Jones said through a mask of grime.

"But that means that the Fascists can't get to us, either," I said.

"I just hope this passage leads somewhere," my father commented.

We followed the passage for what seemed like hours and it led us ever downward. As our torches began to flicker, we heard a low, deep, roaring noise. Hurrying around a last corner, we found a vast underground river spread before us.

"Jones, look!" cried my father. There, next to the river, was a great boat. Covered with gold and silver and precious gems, it sat untouched by time.

"It's a funeral boat," said Jones, running his hands over a terrifying, manlike form with a fox head.

"Annubis, the god that guards the underworld," said Jones as he stroked the horrible creature.

"It's a boat fit for a queen," said my father. "It proves that Sheba's tomb is down here somewhere."

"Roger, old boy, how do you feel about a boat ride?" asked Jones. "We can load old Annubis on board and set sail. My guess is that this river comes out at the foot of the plateau. If we stash the boat in a ravine, hike to the coast, and get some supplies, we can come back for it. Once we're back in New York, we can lay our plans for a proper expedition. This war can't last forever."

"But, Jones," my father said hesitantly. "It's

a priceless museum piece. We can't use it to escape. That would be sacrilege."

"Roger, it's a boat. And as I see it, it's our only way out. You can stay here worshiping its beauty until you die next to it. Or we can use it to get out of here. And if the gods are with us, we'll make it."

And we did!

THE END.

"I've never ridden a camel before," I said nervously as the shaggy, bad-smelling beast stared down at me in contempt.

"You'll get used to it." Jones tugged on his camel's reins and it knelt obediently in the dust before him. Swinging astride, he mounted the huge creature.

Trying to ignore the circle of grinning natives, I imitated him. But my camel only snorted at me and refused to move.

"You got to show him who's boss, kid," said Jones. Smacking the camel with a stick, he forced it to kneel so I could mount.

As we headed into the desert my camel turned and looked at me. The evil expression on its face was a promise that my troubles had just begun.

We rode all day and made camp that evening next to a low, rocky hill. Although we had brought provisions with us, Jones climbed the rocks and used his whip to bring down three rabbitlike creatures.

"Hyraxes," said Jones, showing me how to skin and clean them. "It's better to live off the land and save your supplies for when you really need them."

We roasted the animals over a small fire and washed them down with hot tea.

Jones woke me before dawn, and we mounted the grumbling camels and continued our trek north. Drifting sand gave way to stony soil and scrubby brush. Once we saw people and rode to investigate. But all we found was a hut made of flattened kerosene cans, a tiny spring, and a stunted garden.

"Where did they go?" I asked, standing high in my stirrups, searching the horizon.

"Hiding," grunted Jones as he allowed the camels to drink. "They're afraid."

"Of what?" I asked as we rode away.

"Everything. Bandits. Fascists. It's a rough country, kid. You either fight to keep what's yours, or you run away."

As we rode, Jones flushed quail out of the brush and then dispatched them with his whip. Once, when I dismounted to pick up a bird, my camel snaked its head forward and bit me on the shoulder. Only the heavy folds of my native robes protected me from a painful bite. Furious, I turned and struck it on its nose. Bellowing angrily, it glared at me; brandishing my stick, I glared back.

"That's the way to do it, kid," chuckled Jones. "You'll be a camel driver yet."

The camel sulked along after that but gave me no more trouble. I was quite pleased with myself by the time Jones called a halt. We dismounted below a stony ridge, and Jones built a small fire out of shrubs, which gave off a thin thread of greasy black smoke.

"Best try to sleep now," Jones muttered as he pulled his robes around him and curled up into a ball. "We'll travel later when it cools off."

I was almost asleep when my camel brayed

loudly. I was annoyed, then startled when I felt the thunder of hoofbeats through the dirt beneath my head.

"Get up, kid!" Jones shouted as he reached for his whip. "We got company!"

I scrambled to my feet as eight riders, armed with swords, spears, and rifles, raced over the ridge. Screaming fiercely, they slid their horses down the slope and circled us at a gallop.

"Who are they? What do they want?" I cried as I clutched at Jones's arm.

"Shiftas. Desert bandits," Jones said grimly as he shook me away and uncoiled his whip. "And they want whatever we've got."

"But we'll die without supplies!"

"Maybe," said Jones as he turned, keeping his eyes on the circling riders.

"What do we do?" I asked fearfully.

....

1. *"We're outnumbered, but we can fight, and hope we win." Turn to page 48.*

2. *"Give up, give them what they want, and walk away from this alive." Go on to page 47.*

46

"Your father will never forgive me if I get you killed," Jones muttered.

"I won't get killed!" I cried. "Come on, Jones, let's run them off. There are only eight of them!"

"Believe me, kid, I'd like nothing better. But I can't take chances with your life." Throwing down his pistol, Jones called out to the bandits.

Grinning widely through stained and broken teeth, the bandits approached. Seeing that Jones offered no opposition, they quickly loaded all our possessions onto our camels and rode off laughing.

At the crest of the ridge my camel looked back at me, curled its lip, and added its hideous bray to their laughter.

"Never did like camels," said Jones, kicking a rock.

"We could have fought them off."

"I already told you, kid. I just couldn't take the chance of either one of us getting hurt or killed. This way, at least we're both alive."

Turn to page 18.

Whip cracking and pistol blazing, Jones felled several of the bandits in the first few seconds of their attack.

I snatched Jones's rifle from its scabbard and, trying to steady my shaking hands, fired at the man who led the charge. I missed, but the bullet struck a boulder in front of him and a spray of rock splinters flew into his horse's face. Screaming, the horse reared and fell backward on top of him. Then it scrambled to its feet and ran off into the desert.

Seeing their leader lying crumpled and still, the bandits realized that the fight was lost. They

hauled up their dead and vanished as quickly as they had appeared.

"Good shooting, kid," Jones said as he quickly reloaded his pistol. "We surprised them. They weren't expecting us to be so tough. It was you grabbing that rifle that did it. You're okay!"

My face flushed a bright red. Smiling foolishly, I started packing our gear.

Although we kept careful watch, the bandits did not reappear. Late the next day we reached Addis Ababa.

Turn to page 50.

Tired, dirty, and saddlesore, we passed through the huge wooden gates of Addis Ababa and were faced with the most incredible mix of humanity I had ever seen.

Enormous black men dressed in rough furs, small, slender men swathed in white cloth, and nobles wrapped in silk, carrying fringed parasols, mixed with Fascist soldiers wearing crisp brown uniforms. Donkeys, camels, cows, horses, and dogs threaded through the crush of people.

Pulling our camels behind us, we joined the jostling crowd. Suddenly my camel heaved a great sigh and sat down in the middle of the road. We pulled, yelled, and coaxed, to no avail. Soon a crowd gathered and began to shout advice.

"Camels!" cursed Jones as he drew back his whip. "We've got to get him going. We can't afford this kind of attention."

And then disaster struck. Somehow Jones's whip caught the leg of a warrior, and when he yanked forward, the warrior was pulled with it. Jones, the warrior, and the camel all wound up in a pile together. The camel leaned forward, plucked the lion's-mane headdress off the warrior's head, and ate it!

"You have insulted me!" roared the warrior. "And your beast has eaten my family crest. I demand satisfaction!"

"It was an accident," argued Jones.

"You are a coward!" yelled the warrior.

"I'm no coward," snarled Jones. "How much

will it take to soothe your sense of honor?" and he began counting coins.

The warrior knocked the money out of Jones's hands and drew a sword. "Your life is the cost of my honor!" he shouted.

The crowd murmured its approval. Then the camel leaned over, plucked Jones's headcloth off his head, and started to chew.

"Fascisto!" hissed the warrior as he realized Jones was not a native.

"I'm no Fascist!" Jones yelled, but his voice was lost in the roar of the crowd as the warrior's sword sliced down. Jones ducked and struck out with his whip. It wound itself around the warrior's arm. The warrior grabbed the whip and

reeled Jones in. Screaming encouragement, the crowd closed in around them.

Suddenly there was silence. A Fascist officer and two soldiers pushed through the crowd.

"There is to be no fighting! Seize those men!" said the officer.

"Wait!" I cried. "They're only wrestling!" And turning to Jones and the warrior, I hissed, "Quick! Pretend you're friends or we'll all go to jail!"

The thought of a Fascist jail was more powerful than their dislike for each other; rising to their feet, Jones and the warrior exchanged false smiles and patted each other on the back.

"Who are you?" asked the officer, eyeing Jones suspiciously. Jones babbled and grinned foolishly.

"Please, sir," I said in Italian. "My brother is not bright but means no harm. With your permission, I'll take him home."

The officer made a noise of disgust. Gesturing to his men, he pushed his way back through the silent crowd and climbed into a large black touring car. And there, to my amazement, sat my father! We stared at each other helplessly until the car drove away.

"Jones!" I gasped. "My father was in that car! We've got to go after him!"

"Take it easy, kid," whispered Jones. "We can't just run after them. Give me a minute— I'll think of something."

"You not Fascisto?" asked the warrior.

"I told you we weren't," snarled Jones. "But you wouldn't listen."

"You want man in car?"

"Yes, we want him," I replied. "He's my father. The Fascists kidnapped him and brought him here. Can you help us?"

"Fascisto killed my father," growled the warrior, "and put my brothers in jail. I will help you!" Then, striding to the camel, he thumped it soundly and dragged it to its feet.

....

1. *"Let us go to jail now,"* he said with a murderous look on his face. Turn to page 54.

2. *"I think we should wait until night,"* argued Jones. Turn to page 57.

"How can we get inside in broad daylight?" asked Jones.

"I, Kassaye, second son of Auri the Lion, have a plan," said our new friend, and looping his arms through ours, he pulled us into the bazaar.

Haggling and cajoling, he bought a dozen plump chickens, baskets of vegetables, and a sack of freshly baked bread. He piled it all upon a newly purchased cart and then wrapped a new headcloth around Jones's head. Then we set off for the Fascist camp.

Hiding our weapons under our robes, we drove up to the camp gates. Acting the fool, Kassaye asked such ridiculously low prices for his foodstuffs that the guards waved us toward the kitchens, shaking their heads at our stupidity.

As we walked I spotted the car standing in front of an open doorway.

"Jones, Kassaye, look!" I whispered. "It's the car!" Without missing a step, Kassaye turned the cart and barreled up the steps, through the doorway, and into the room.

"What the...! *Out!*" roared the officer who sat behind the desk. But I was not listening. Seated in a chair in front of the desk was my father!

Jones was at the officer's side before he could move. "Be quiet," he snarled, jamming the muzzle of his rifle under the officer's chin, "or I'll kill you!"

The man froze.

Jones ripped the belt off his robes, tied him up firmly, and gagged him with his headcloth.

"Jones! George!" my father cried weakly. "I can't believe you're really here!"

"Save it for later, Roger. We've still got to get away." Then, in one swift motion, he ripped the drapes down from the windows and wrapped them around my father. "You might pass for a native if no one looks too closely. Okay, let's go."

The four of us walked down the steps, pushing the cart in front of us. But instead of turning toward the gates, Kassaye walked in the opposite direction.

"Where are you going? We've got to leave!" Jones whispered.

"Brothers!" hissed Kassaye.

"This won't work a second time! Let's leave now and think of another plan," urged Jones. But Kassaye kept walking.

"What's this all about, Jones?" asked my father.

"Honor," muttered Jones. After a moment's hesitation he followed Kassaye.

The jail was easy to spot. There were two guards posted at the entrance. Kassaye attempted to push his cart past them, but they barred his way with their rifles.

"We were told to deliver this food here," I said, hoping to ease the way.

"Who told you?" demanded a guard. I stammered and tried to bluff, but Kassaye was impatient. Shrieking a war cry, he ripped his sword out of its scabbard and killed the closest guard.

Things were a blur after that. Jones used his whip and his rifle, and I tried to use the pistol but lost it before I could fire a shot. My father picked up a rock and felled at least one soldier, but none of it did any good. It wasn't long before we were surrounded by soldiers and overcome.

So now Jones and Kassaye and I are sitting in a cell and the commandant has my father again. Kassaye's brothers are down the hall from us and Kassaye tells me there is a plan. We can't give up, I know that. I just hope this plan is better than the last one and that it's not really...

THE END.

"I, Kassaye, have a plan," said the warrior as he strode into the bazaar, leaving us to follow. Squatting on the hard sun-baked earth, we watched as he haggled with a toothless old man. Finally a deal was struck, and smiling broadly, the old man crossed his hands over his chest and bowed several times.

Smiling and bowing as well, Kassaye said, "Live long and in peace, grandfather. We will return at nightfall."

"What was that all about?" demanded Jones as the three of us left the bazaar and settled down at a café table in the shade of a large tree.

Smiling wickedly, Kassaye ignored him and spoke at great length with a small ragged child who appeared at our table. Finally Jones gave up and sat fuming.

"Addis Ababa is very interesting town," Kassaye said innocently. "You must visit palace and monument before you leave."

"What monument?" I asked idly.

"Oh, very old monument to dead queen," he replied.

"*What?*" yelled Jones, sitting bolt upright. "Where is it? Take us to it!"

"Oh, no," Kassaye said, shaking his massive head. "I only joking. It is forbidden. It is cursed. Death strikes any who dare to enter."

"That's crazy," snapped Jones. "All over the world people are looting burial sites. What's so special about this one?"

"It is cursed!" Kassaye insisted stubbornly, and only the arrival of the little boy, bearing platters of food, kept them from a major argument.

As we ate the hot, spicy food, Kassaye held up a glass full of amber fluid. "Tej," he said with a grin, and offered it to us. I took a tiny sip of the stuff and began to cough and splutter.

"What is it?" I choked.

"Native home brew," gasped Jones. "Knocks the top of your head off in ten minutes."

"Tej will get us into Fascisto camp tonight. Then we free family," said Kassaye, smiling. "And maybe we break some heads."

"Okay!" said Jones. "But that's still eight hours away."

. . . .

1. *"Why don't we check out this burial site until then. I mean, it can't hurt if we just look, can it?"* Go on to page 59.

2. *"No,"* thundered Kassaye. *"Is cursed! Family more important. We stick to plan!"* Turn to page 62.

"Kassaye will not go into monument," the warrior said stubbornly. "It is cursed!"

Jones leaned back in his chair, lit a cigar, and blew out a cloud of blue smoke. "Yeah," he said, studying the end of his cigar, "I guess you can't help it if you're a coward. Probably runs in the family."

Kassaye leaped to his feet, sword in hand. "You dare call me a coward! You dare insult family honor!" he cried, his face contorted in rage. "I kill you! Kassaye not afraid of nothing!"

Jones did not even flinch. Raising his eyes to the infuriated warrior, he said, "You just said you were afraid to enter the tomb. Don't know why, nothing there but bones and dust. Guess it'll be just me and the kid. He's not afraid." Rising to his feet, Jones stretched slowly. Then he grabbed his pack and my arm and we walked away. "Don't look back," hissed Jones.

Seconds later Kassaye was at my side. "You never find tomb. This wrong way. I, Kassaye, the lion of the desert, who fears *nothing*, will show you the right way."

Jones winked at me, and we turned and followed Kassaye, the lion of the desert.

It stood almost in the very center of town and rose straight up into the air, a smooth pillar of unbroken stone. Jones whistled through his teeth as he stared up at it. Reading the hieroglyphics carved on it, he circled it twice before he spoke.

"Tenth century B.C., or I'm a dogfish. Think I've seen one like this before in Egypt." He positioned the camels so that they screened us, then fiddled with the carvings. It took him a while before he got it right. But just as Kassaye was beginning to fidget, there was a rough rumbling and a slab of stone slid aside. Dry, musty air engulfed us as the blackness within was revealed for the first time in centuries.

"Why hasn't anyone done this before?" I

asked nervously as we entered the monolith. "I mean it's not very well hidden."

"You heard Kassaye. There's a powerful curse on the place. People here still believe it after three thousand years."

The stone slab shut behind us. Jones struck a light, and we walked through the narrow tunnel. It led us downward for a long time. Then, far in the distance, there was a glimmer of light.

"Look," said Jones, "it divides here."

. . . .

1. *"The right-hand tunnel goes up, and there's light at the end."* Turn to page 66.

2. *"The left-hand branch continues down."* Turn to page 69.

Jones raged, begged, and argued, but nothing he said changed Kassaye's mind. Finally Jones gave up and brooded in silence for the rest of the long afternoon. When night fell, Kassaye rose from under the tree where he had slept. Dusting off his furs, he gestured for us to follow and we returned to the bazaar.

Grinning toothlessly, the old man welcomed us and, bowing deeply, opened a set of wooden doors. Standing in a small courtyard was a wagon filled with barrels. Kassaye climbed onto the wagon, checked the contents of the barrels, and smiled.

Somehow we persuaded the camels to pull the wagon, and it lurched slowly toward the Fascist camp.

"Halt and identify!" cried the sentry.

Kassaye leaped down and scurried over to the guard. Cringing and bowing, he said, "It is only me, Rusef, lowly worm of the desert, delivering the gift."

"What gift?" growled the guard.

"Why, it is your commandant's birthday! He ordered these barrels of tej beer for his men so they might join in celebrating his birth. Did he not say? I was to be here hours ago, but my unworthy wagon broke. Perhaps I could just leave the wagon with you and you could see that the men drink. Then commandant will not holler at Rusef."

"Birthday? Tej?" the guard said suspiciously as he tasted the sample Kassaye held out to him. "Well, all right. Leave it here and I'll take care of it. I know what it's like to have him mad at you. Strange that he would do this."

Leaving the wagon, Kassaye, Jones, and I drove the camels out of the camp.

"Good job, Kassaye," whispered Jones. "In an hour every soldier in the place will either be drunk or asleep."

"Oh, much sooner," Kassaye said with a quiet laugh. "I add something extra to the tej."

And so it was that thirty minutes later we strolled back into camp and, stepping over the soldiers who lay collapsed at their posts, freed my father, Kassaye's family, and everyone else we could find.

"Jones! George!" said my father. "Thank God, you're here! They know about the laser and the treasure, too! Every day they take me down into the tunnels and try to make me tell them where it is. I've played dumb so far, but I know it's down there! Jones, we've got to find it before we leave!"

Jones pushed my father into one of the large canvas-covered trucks. I climbed up behind them.

"Roger, you're crazy," Jones said as he hot-wired the ignition. "Any second now someone's going to figure out what's happened and then all hell will break loose. Not everyone drank that stuff."

As if to prove his words, sirens began to wail, dogs began to bark, and three men with rifles came running out of the main building.

"Down!" screamed Jones. The engine rumbled into life, he threw the truck into reverse, and we squealed out of the compound. Above me there was the sound of shattering glass, and splinters rained down upon us.

1. "Jones, if we go down into that maze of tunnels, no one will ever think to look for us there." Turn to page 34.

2. "Roger, our government needs that laser. If we're all dead or prisoners in some Fascist camp, they'll never get it. We've got to leave—now!" Turn to page 33.

Jones told Squint we had decided to catch the train to Addis Ababa.

"I wishes you would change your minds and stay with us," said Squint, "but if you will not, then we will come with you. Is too dangerous for you to travels alone."

"Oh, no. We wouldn't hear of it," Jones said smoothly. "We know how important your pilgrimage is to you. Don't worry about us. We'll be fine without you."

"But, but…" Squint stammered feebly. But there was really nothing he could say, and we left the two of them fuming in frustration as we walked away.

Fortunately, Jones had slept with his money belt on and we were able to purchase food from other pilgrims.

We reentered the desert, and I welcomed its openness with relief. As we trudged back toward the railroad Jones said, "I feel much better about this, kid. Your dad would never forgive me if I got you killed. We should be safe enough once we get to the train."

....

Turn to page 16.

Kassaye followed close behind me. I could feel him tremble and once I heard his teeth chatter. His fear was infectious. Soon my stomach began to flutter.

"Jones, why don't we check out the light?" I asked.

"Okay, kid. Why not?" said Jones. And turning right, we hurried toward the light.

When we finally reached it, we found that the light was filtering up through the floor of the passage.

"This is strange," muttered Jones. He bent down to examine the floor. "George? Kassaye? Do you hear voices?"

As the three of us huddled together, there was a soft, slithery noise and then the floor collapsed beneath us! Arms waving wildly, the three of us plunged through the gaping hole and fell into a lighted room. We staggered to our feet gasping and choking and saw a terrible sight. Fascists! We were surrounded by them.

Before we could reach for our weapons, we were seized and searched.

"This is most odd," said the commandant. "Take them away and lock them up. No one breaks into a prison! They are either fools or enemies. We shall find out which and deal with them accordingly."

As we were being led away I heard the commandant say, "Lieutenant, this could be what we've been looking for. That hole must be part of the tunnel system under the obelisk. It could lead us to Sheba's treasure. Once we find

the treasure, we can force the doctor to reveal the laser plans. Then victory will be ours!"

I quickly translated for Jones as we were bustled down a brightly lit hall. His eyes burned with anger and there were two red spots high on his cheekbones.

"Victory?" he said between clenched teeth. "Not if I can help it!"

THE END.

"It's probably just a landfall," said Jones, looking at the light. "Let's go left."

And so we turned left, into the darkness. I was scared, and rightly so. Twice Jones found traps that could have killed us. Once we had to work our way around a massive rock fall and all that remained of two crushed skeletons.

Finally Jones halted in front of what appeared to be a blank wall. Running his fingers over the rock, he pressed, pulled, and poked, and then, to my amazement, the wall groaned and swung inward.

Kassaye hissed with fright and refused to enter the darkness that lay beyond.

Holding the lantern high, Jones and I entered the room. We were met by a light so bright that we were forced to shield our eyes. Peering cautiously between my fingers, I beheld an astounding sight—row after row of mirror-bright shields, standing upright and reflecting the light of our lantern back into our eyes. We moved slowly forward and saw an even more amazing sight. Standing there, wearing gold helmets and armor, clutching gold-tipped spears in their skeletal fingers, was an ancient army fit for a queen. A dead queen.

Threading our way through the dead ranks, we passed into a second, larger room.

"Well, kid, looks like we hit the jackpot," said Jones as he looked around him. And I could not argue.

Jewel-filled caskets, bars of gold and silver,

gilded furniture, and other magnificent offerings were piled high in the frescoed chambers.

Gesturing at the proud face painted on one of the walls, Jones said, "I don't think there's any question—we've found the treasure of Sheba."

"Is she here somewhere?" I asked.

"Somewhere," answered Jones. "There are probably a lot more rooms like this. But they'll keep. In a few years the war will be over and we can come back." He scooped a handful of gems from the nearest cask and placed them in his pocket.

"If Kassaye's plan doesn't work, we can use these to buy your father out. There's always a way if you've got enough money. Here, kid, take this," said Jones, flipping me a small gold object. It was a scarab, a beetle believed to bring good luck, inset with rubies.

"I take back everything I said in New York, kid. You've been a real trouper. Your father should be proud of you. And now why don't we go and tell him so?"

THE END.

"Tell me more about Lalibela," Jones said as our ship neared the Red Sea port of Assam.

Leaning on the rail, watching gulls race by, I tried to remember what I had read.

"I'm sure you know that Ethiopians are Christians and have been since the eleventh century. Well, Lalibela is the religious center of the country.

"It's all volcanic rock there, and when they built a church, they dug out a big courtyard, leaving a huge square chunk of rock in the middle. Then they carved doors and windows in the rock and hollowed it out. Everything is carved into it, pews, altars, rooms, statues. There are ten rock churches in all. My father thinks the area is honeycombed with tunnels. It's the perfect place to hide a treasure."

We docked later that day and by the next morning had purchased mules, supplies, and native robes and were on our way.

"Why are so many people on the roads?" Jones asked, drawing his robe across his face to block out the dust.

"It's almost Christmas," I replied. "They're making a pilgrimage to Lalibela."

"Well, that's good news," Jones said. "No one will even notice us in this crowd. We'll just be two more faces." Later that day, as we sat in the meager shade of a boulder and ate a lunch of dried dates, onion, and cheese, we were approached by two men, one of whom squinted badly.

71

"Good afternoons, honorable sirs," said the man with the squint.

"We are going to Lalibela same as you and I says to Fredo, my esteemable companion, how nice it would be to journey in the company of other educated gentlemens such as ourselves. Why don't we travel together, for safety as well as pleasures? Soon we will be great friends."

I stared at the squinty, grinning fellow and his hulking companion in amazement. How did they know we were going to Lalibela? We had told no one! How had they known we were not natives? Jones and I were both dressed in flowing robes. Something was wrong!

To my astonishment, Jones, who had listened politely, nodded and said, "Sounds like a good idea to me. Why are you folks going to Lalibela?"

"Because we are religious persons," said Squint, putting his hands together and gazing piously upward.

How could Jones buy this man's story? Not even a child would believe it! I rose to my feet, intending to speak out, when a swift warning look from Jones stopped me.

Soon after, our two new companions were helping themselves to our food supplies, and Jones motioned me to join him.

As he rearranged the mule's pack I whispered, "Why did you let them come? Surely you don't believe their story! Look at them. They're not pilgrims!"

"Keep your voice down. Of course they're not pilgrims. The squinty one has been with us since New York. Don't turn around! And listen to me! Would you rather have them here where we can keep an eye on them, or creeping around behind us, up to no good?"

"I guess that makes sense," I said grudgingly. "But I don't like them."

"I'm not asking you to adopt them, kid. Just be civil. It's all part of the game and you agreed to play by my rules."

I tried to conceal my dislike, and we traveled together until we reached the foot of the great plateau that led to Lalibela. Our companions, who had done little but eat, drink, sleep, and avoid chores, rode up to speak with Jones.

"How do you go, Mr. Jones?" asked Squint.

· ·

1. *"I plan to follow the other travelers up this dry riverbed."* Turn to page 74.

2. *"Fredo and me, we knows a quicker route. Come with us."* Turn to page 95.

"I think we'll follow the pilgrims," said Jones. "Shortcuts can be dangerous."

Squint and Fredo protested loudly, but they could not change Jones's mind.

We traveled up the dry riverbed all that day. After the heat of the desert, it was cool and pleasant. Off to our left we could hear the rush of water.

"Irrigation channels," said Squint, "so the peoples can grow crops all year."

Fredo's mule began to limp after lunch, and by dark we had fallen far behind the group of pilgrims we had been following.

As Jones and I rolled up in our blankets next to the campfire, Squint and Fredo rose to their feet.

"We purify us and pray tonight," Squint said. "You sleep best. We sees you in the morning."

"It'll take more than prayer to purify them," muttered Jones, closing his eyes.

I don't know how long I had been asleep when the ground began to tremble beneath me and our mules started to bray hysterically.

"George! On your feet!" yelled Jones.

I sat up sleepily, trying to figure out what was happening.

"Run, George! Run!" Jones shouted.

Stumbling to my feet, I followed him as he dashed for the nearest bank. But I was still stupid with sleep and had barely reached it when I heard a deep growling rumble. Looking up, I saw an immense wall of black water thundering down on me. The mules, outlined in the embers of the fire, reared and tugged at their ropes. Seconds later they were swallowed up by the water. I heard Jones yelling at me from above as the water hit the campfire, and then it was on me.

I felt like I had been hit by a truck. Kicking and waving my arms as water poured down my throat, I surfaced once and sank again. This time there was a terrible tightness across my chest. *So this is what it's like to drown*, I thought. The grip on my chest grew tighter. Then something took hold of my hair and pulled.

My head came out of the water, and in spite

of the pain in my chest I drew a deep breath. And then, scraping over rocks and branches, I was pulled to safety.

Jones clutched me to him. Then he flopped me over and pounded on my back. Water poured out of me. I was a sorry mess, but I was alive.

By morning the flood had dwindled and stopped. Our supplies were gone. We found the body of one of our mules downstream. We never found the other.

We were salvaging some of our supplies from the dead mule when Squint and Fredo reappeared.

"Oh, how happy you are still alive!" said Squint. Fredo looked anything but happy.

"Where were you when this happened?" Jones asked softly.

"We was praying," Squint said quickly.

Jones turned his back on them. "We were lucky last night, kid," he said. "By all the odds, we should be dead."

....

1. "Maybe we should lose these characters. They're dangerous. We can intercept the train to Addis Ababa if we turn aside here." Turn to page 65.

2. "It's all right," I said. "I'm not afraid. We can keep on going." Go on to page 77.

"It takes more than that to scare me!" I said angrily.

"Are you sure?" asked Jones, looking at me intently. "I'd like to check out Lalibela. But it wouldn't be worth it if you were dead. Your dad would never forgive me if I got you killed."

"I wouldn't like it too much either. No, let's keep going. I have a feeling this is where they would take my dad."

"Okay, kid, you're on," said Jones. He turned to Squint and told him we would continue.

"Excellent!" cried Squint. "Excellent!"

We traveled all that morning, stopping only to examine the dam that had loosed the flood. Workers swarmed over its face, repairing the damage that Jones said could only have been caused by dynamite.

"Shocking!" murmured Squint, but for an instant I saw a faint smile on Fredo's face.

The workers lived nearby, and Jones was able to buy mules to replace the ones we had lost.

As he counted out the silver from his money belt, a look of intense greed crossed Fredo's face and I decided to watch him closely.

Later that afternoon we spotted some ruins high on a hill.

"Portuguese," said Jones. "Sixteenth century."

Soon after, the walls of the riverbed rose up on each side of us until they were far above our heads. The trail grew narrower and narrower until we were forced to ride single file, with Jones and me in the lead.

We were approaching a great rock that jutted out over the trail when there was a sharp cracking noise. I stopped to look and was startled to see Jones hurl himself at me. Before I could react, we crashed to the ground, with Jones on top.

"What's going on?" I gasped, but my words were lost in a loud explosion. Jones did not stop to answer. He shoved me into a narrow undercut in the bank and crammed himself in after me. Seconds later I felt the shock of several more explosions and the thud of falling rock. Finally there was silence and Jones rolled aside.

We stared around us in shock. The great rock outcrop was gone—pulverized into pieces. The riverbed was filled with debris.

"I didn't think they'd give up easily," Jones said grimly, "but I thought they'd wait till night."

"What do you mean?"

"Our pals. They must have set this charge last night and triggered it by some sort of hand-held device as we rode up. It's a lucky thing they're so bad at this or we'd be dead."

We got to our feet and I saw that Jones's robes were torn and stained with blood.

"Jones! You're hurt!"

"I'm okay, kid, which is more than I can say for the mules."

And once more we were afoot.

"Where do you think they are?" I asked as we picked our way back down the riverbed.

"Close. They'll want to check their work, but they'll give the buzzards and hyenas time, in case we're only injured."

I shivered. "Then why are we trying to find them?"

"They're fools and bunglers, but they've almost killed us twice. It's time to stop them."

We found them at dusk. Thinking us dead, they had camped in the ruins and lit a great fire. We watched as they roasted a goat and lolled in front of the fire with a jar of native beer.

They were thick with drink when we walked into camp.

"Mr. Jones! Mr. George! We think you are dead!" cried Squint, staggering to his feet. "Fredo and me, we tries to find your body, but we cannot. We think the avalanche bury you!"

"Avalanche, huh?" snarled Jones.

Then, out of the corner of my eye, I saw Fredo's hand move.

"Jones, look out!" I screamed as Fredo's arm came up holding a knife.

So quickly that I wasn't even sure I had seen it, Jones drew his pistol with one hand, his whip with the other. The whip cracked forward and wrapped around Squint. A bullet sent Fredo screaming to the ground.

It was over. Jones disarmed the pair of them, muffled their cries with their own robes, and tied them up.

After going through their supplies, we cleaned Jones's wounds, and he changed into a set of Fredo's clothes. Then we set upon the roasted meat and had soon picked the carcass clean.

Finally Jones kicked dirt over the fire, and we led Fredo's and Squint's mules into the night.

"Jones, what will happen to them?" I asked.

"They'll be found," said Jones as he swung up onto the mule.

"By whom?"

"By their friends, or by the hyenas. It all depends on who gets there first."

Turn to page 82.

It took us another week to reach Lalibela, but the roads were thick with pilgrims and there were no more attempts on our lives.

As we entered the red walls of the city, Jones wrapped his robe around his face so that only his eyes were visible. I followed his example.

"Fascists!" hissed Jones. Glancing around, I saw that there were soldiers everywhere.

"What are we going to do?"

"Let me think for a minute," said Jones. Pulling the mules into an empty courtyard, he pondered the problem.

....

1. *"There's safety in numbers. We can stay with the pilgrims until we get a chance to explore." Turn to page 104.*

2. *"Or we could just brazen it out. Even if they do spot us, they're not going to start trouble with Americans." Go on to page 83.*

"I never did like sneaking around," said Jones. "Let's just do it." We turned the mules around and rode back into the street.

There was a platoon of soldiers marching smartly down the road. We stopped in front of them, and Jones had me speak to the lieutenant who led them.

"Good afternoon," I said in Italian. "Where can we find your commandant?"

He looked at us suspiciously. Then, pointing back the way we had come, he said, "There is a large mountain outside of town. You will find him there." Thanking him politely, we rode away.

When we got to the mountain, we set our mules upon the narrow trail that wound up its steep walls. We came around a sharp turn and to my surprise I saw my father standing with the commandant. Below them several men were digging in the hard, red volcanic soil.

Jones pulled me back before we were seen. Crouching together against the side of the mountain, we argued about what to do:

....

1. *"Let's just go in there and get him," I argued. "There aren't that many soldiers. We can do it. I know we can." Turn to page 84.*

2. *Indy said, "Let's wait until they leave, follow them, and break him out of wherever they're holding him." Turn to page 86.*

83

"You're right, kid. There aren't that many of them. And most of them are down in those trenches. We'll have them at a disadvantage. C'mon!" We dashed around the bend and pointed our guns at them.

"Freeze!" I said in Italian. "And no one will get hurt."

"Jones! George!" cried my father as he ran toward us. "Thank God, you've come! It's here! The treasure! I've found it!"

My father and I helped Jones herd the Fascists into the trench, laughing and talking as we did so.

I guess that was our downfall. We were paying so little attention to anyone but our-

selves that we never even heard the soldiers until it was too late.

"You will stop, please!" said a harsh voice. Turning, we saw the cold-eyed lieutenant and his entire platoon standing above us with guns drawn.

So here we are in a prison in Lalibela, wondering if this is truly

THE END.

Jones finally persuaded me that it would be a mistake to try to rescue my dad without a better plan. But even though I knew he was right, I sulked like a five-year-old all the way down the mountain. It was only when we were hiding in a grove of trees and I saw the cold-eyed lieutenant and his men creep silently up the mountain that I knew Jones had been right. Had we stayed, we would have been caught. Shamefaced, I apologized.

"Don't mention it, kid. Hard as it is to believe, I've made a few mistakes in my time. Be quiet now. They'll be down soon." He was right. The lieutenant and his soldiers filed down the mountain, and in their center marched my father.

Joining a group of pilgrims, we followed the soldiers back to town without being spotted.

"Excellent!" said Jones as my father and the commandant entered a large adobe building near the center of town. "It's always easier to kidnap someone with lots of people around. Now let's get to work."

We walked through town and Jones talked with rogues and priests and pilgrims. A lot of money changed hands. "It's Christmas, call it charity," said Jones as he shook the last hand and smiled cheerfully. Then we traded our mules for three horses whose owner said they would run like the wind.

By nightfall strange wailing music filled the air. "Good," said Jones, nodding at the throbbing drumbeat. "Sounds like the place is filling up."

As we led the horses into the crowded street it seemed as though the number of pilgrims had doubled, and we pushed our way through with great difficulty.

When we reached the appointed spot, we found the rogues, the royally robed priests with their drum-carrying servants, and a horde of white-robed pilgrims waiting for us as arranged.

"Confusion!" said Jones, smiling broadly. Then he gave the signal and we all moved out. Singing loudly, waving brass braziers of sweet incense, and pounding their drums, the crowd surged down the street. But as we drew even with the adobe building, the swaying, chanting procession turned aside and pushed through the door.

The crowd filled the small building to capacity and the singing, the drums, the smell of incense, and the smoking torches soon became overwhelming. Sweat ran down my face and I felt myself grow dizzy.

There were brief cries as the astonished guards were overpowered by Jones and his hired henchmen.

The crowd continued to mill about creating havoc until Jones gave the signal, and then we spilled out of the building and continued down the street.

"There, that should fix them," Jones said

with a happy grin on his face. "I bet they *never* figure out what just happened."

"What *did* happen, Jones?" I asked in total confusion. "Did we do it?"

And then a pilgrim walking next to Jones pushed back his head robes. It was my father! Our plan had succeeded.

My father and I hugged each other, unable to speak. "Look," said Jones, "I hate to break up the reunion, but we have a decision to make:

....

1. *"The guards will be discovered soon, and then all hell is going to break loose. I suggest we get on those horses and get out of here."* Go on to page 89.

2. *"We can't, Jones. I know where the treasure is," said my father. "We have to stay."* Turn to page 90.

"Jones, we're so close! We can't leave," argued my father. "Think of the treasure!"

"Look, Roger, we're alive now, right? Well, I'd like to stay alive," said Jones as he lifted me up onto a horse.

"Use your head, Roger. Treasure is only metal and stone. Is it as important as your kid? Normally I'm as greedy as the next man, but if I had a kid, I wouldn't risk him. Especially not this one. If I liked kids, I'd say he was a winner!"

"You're right, of course," my dad said, and got on his horse without another word.

It was a long hard ride back to the Red Sea. We rode by night and slept by day. The Fascists didn't give up easily, but neither did we, and in the end we made it.

As the rusty tramp steamer puffed its way out of the harbor, my father leaned on the rail and looked back at the dim outline of the purple plateau. "One of these days, Jones, you and I will come back here and find that treasure."

"Don't forget about me," I said. "It just so happens that I know a lot about Ethiopia. I could be a big help!"

Jones ruffled my hair. "Kid, when that day comes, you'll be at the top of the list."

THE END.

"Listen, Jones, the first thing they'd expect us to do is ride for the coast. I think we should stay here and let them go off on a wild goose chase. I know a place where they'll never find us," said my dad.

"That's not a bad idea," mused Jones. Then, turning to three tough-looking men who stood behind him, he told them the new plan. They shook their heads and backed away until Jones pressed more silver coins into their hands.

Finally the deal was struck, and the three men took our horses and rode out of town.

"They'll be seen and followed. But by the time the Fascists catch up with them, we'll be gone," said Jones. "Now, where is this place?"

"Follow me," said my dad, and he plunged into the crowd.

We followed him with difficulty because the streets were packed with pilgrims.

"Hurry," whispered my father, and dodging between the white-robed forms, we entered the courtyard of an enormous church. Even in the dark it was impressive.

"This way," whispered my father, and Jones and I followed him into the building. It was very, very dark. Burning braziers hung from the walls, glowing like angry eyes.

My father took one of the braziers down from the wall and pulled open a trap door in the floor behind the massive altar. We all climbed down.

"What is this place?" I asked, touching the

walls that closed in on either side of me. "I don't like it. It's creepy."

"You're not supposed to like it," answered my father. "It represents the descent into hell. It's supposed to scare you into being a better person. By tomorrow it'll be filled with pilgrims."

"You didn't bring us down here for self-improvement, Roger. What's the story?" asked Jones.

"The story is that there isn't anything up on that mountain. I was just leading the Fascists on a wild goose chase.

"As soon as I arrived I noticed that the high priests of these churches had huge gemstones woven into their robes and wore gold ornaments of ancient design."

"But, Roger, that doesn't mean a thing," argued Jones. "This is an ancient kingdom. Did you expect their artifacts to be new?"

"No, of course not. But many of them wear circlets of pure gold engraved with a woman's profile. And I've seen several gold and ivory staffs topped with that same profile. When I tried to examine the pieces, the priests got very upset and avoided me.

"I know I'm right. They've found the treasure of Sheba and hidden it down here. It's a perfect place—most people would be too afraid to come here."

I could understand that. I was certainly afraid. Even though Jones and my dad were right in front of me and we had the brazier to light the way, it was scary. And I kept thinking I heard something behind me. But when I looked, I never saw anything.

The path got narrower and descended more steeply, spiraling deeper and deeper into the earth. The walls were worn smooth by the thousands of hands that had pressed against them over the centuries. At last the path leveled off and we trudged on.

It was Jones who found the square that was cut in the ceiling above us.

"That can't be it," I said. "It's too obvious."

"Pilgrims have to walk this in the dark," my father said. "They'd never see it."

A shudder ran through me. I couldn't imagine walking through here in the dark.

"Here, George, see if you can open it," said Jones, lifting me up till I could reach the trap door. I found the latch, released it, and swung the door down. Then Jones pushed me into the waiting darkness. My dad came next, carrying the brazier, followed by Jones.

As my father raised the brazier we were dazzled by an answering reflection. And then we saw it. Treasure! Heaps and mounds of it. Gems, gold, silver, and jewelry, piled as high and as far as our light would shine.

"I see it, but I don't believe it," whispered my father.

"Believe it," said Jones. "It's real."

"What do we do now?" I asked.

"Take a few small objects and leave. We'll have to get out of the country and wait until this war is over. Then we'll come back and do this right," said Jones.

"It will not be necessary for you to come back," quavered a thin, old voice in English. "For you will never leave."

And then the trap door swung shut. Just before it closed, the voice said, "You have found that which you thought to steal, but the ancients guard their treasure well. Your bones shall help them keep their vigil."

THE END.

"What they say makes sense, kid. Here, look at the map. If we climb the plateau here and then cut over, I bet we'd be in Lalibela three, four days sooner."

"Jones, if that's true why wouldn't everyone go this way?"

"Everyone not mens like us. We very, very brave," said Squint, thumping his chest.

"What's to be brave about? Is it dangerous?" I asked.

Squint shrugged and avoided my eyes. "Little bit of avalanches, that's all."

"Avalanches are nothing to worry about, kid. Just don't make any noise," said Jones. And that was it. In spite of my doubts I had no choice but to get on my mule and follow them. But I decided to watch Squint and Fredo very carefully.

The climb was very steep and the mules tried each step carefully before putting their weight down. There were signs of rock slides all around us. In places, whole sections of the mountain had slid away, leaving raw wounds in the earth.

Shortly after noon Fredo's mule began to give him trouble, sidestepping and refusing to move.

"You go," called Squint. "Maybe he gots a stone in his hoof. We catches up soon."

As Jones and I rode away I felt certain that something was wrong.

The trail grew worse. The ground was sandy and full of small stones that slid under the mules' hoofs. Soon it became necessary for us to dismount and lead them.

We were in the middle of a long, smooth slope when suddenly the ground gave way beneath my feet. I threw myself down, hoping to break my fall, but then the whole stretch of road began to slide.

"Hold on, kid, I'm coming!" yelled Jones, and through the whirl of dirt and stones I saw him running after me.

I tried to hold on, but there was nothing to hold on to. The earth just crumbled away beneath me and I rolled faster and faster down the slope. Everything blurred and then there was an explosion of red and black inside my head.

I woke up to find Jones bending over me.

"My God, kid! What are you trying to do, get yourself killed?"

"But, Jones," I said weakly, "I didn't do it on purpose. It was an accident!"

"That's no excuse!"

I rose shakily and touched my head carefully. There was a large bump at the temple and my fingers came away covered with blood.

"There's a little stream over here," said Jones. "Let's get you cleaned up."

The stream bubbled out of a small cave lined with tiny ferns and mosses. It was so beautiful I could hardly believe it was part of this dry, broken land. Jones and I had just entered the cave when there was a sharp cracking noise that echoed off the walls of the mountain.

"We're in for it now," said Jones. Grabbing my arm, he pulled me into the deepest corner of the cave.

"What's the matter?"

"Avalanche. Listen," he answered.

There was a low, menacing rumble. Then it grew deeper, more intense, and the walls of the cave began to shudder. Tiny pieces of dirt fell on our heads, and the stream stopped flowing. Then it was upon us, roaring like a freight train. Boulders the size of houses bounced down the slopes, and smaller rocks flew through the air like bullets.

At last it ended. We crawled out of the cave and looked around. Everything was different. The slope was scraped clean down to the bedrock. The little cave had saved our lives.

"I should have listened to you, kid," Jones said bitterly. "But I thought it would be okay.

If I ever get my hands on those clowns, I'll tie them in knots."

"What are you talking about?"

"Didn't you hear that sharp cracking noise, right before the avalanche started? That was a rifle shot. Our pals started this on purpose. If you hadn't fallen and we hadn't found this cave, we'd be buried under that rubble right now."

I started to shake then. "Sorry," I managed to say as I tried to control it.

"Don't be sorry, kid," said Jones. "After all, it's not every day a mountain almost falls on you."

Just then there was a gurgling noise and the stream began to flow again. I sank down next to it and poured water over my head.

"Well, kid, what do you think? Should we:

....

1. *"Walk out of here and catch the train to Addis Ababa? I don't really want to take any more chances with your life." Turn to page 16.*

2. *"Or keep going? They probably think we're dead." Turn to page 100.*

We decided to keep going and luck was with us. We worked our way back up the slope and followed what was left of the trail. Suddenly there was a raucous braying and both of our mules, which we had assumed were dead, galloped up. They stuck to us like glue for the rest of the day.

We spent a cold night on the mountain. Once there was a terrible shriek and a burst of hideous laughter. I sat up abruptly, wakened out of an uneasy sleep.

"Go back to sleep, kid," Jones said, and I saw that he was still sitting up holding his rifle. "It's nothing. A lion just caught his dinner and the hyenas are waiting for the leftovers."

I lay back down, drawing the blanket over my head and curling up on the cold, hard ground. Maybe Jones had been right. Maybe I shouldn't have come. Boy Scouts hadn't prepared me for avalanches, broken dams, and people who tried to kill me. My head hurt, my muscles ached, and I wanted to go home.

I woke to the smell of coffee. Warming myself over the small fire that Jones had built, I watched streaks of pink spread across the gray sky and inhaled the cold, sharp air. The fears of the night faded with the first sip of scalding coffee.

We had just finished our coffee when there was a clatter of rocks and Squint and Fredo staggered into camp. Fredo's arm was tied up in rags.

Jones leaped to his feet and grabbed his

rifle. But Fredo and Squint just limped to the fire and collapsed.

"What happened to you?" snarled Jones.

"Avalanche," whispered Squint. "We was right behind you. We was almost killed."

"You need more practice," said Jones. "A good hit man isn't supposed to get caught in his own trap."

But Fredo and Squint did not respond, and for the first time I wondered if Jones and I had been wrong about them.

Jones must have shared my doubts because he said no more, and after giving them coffee, we broke camp and continued on our way.

Fredo and Squint were too tired to give us any trouble and dozed on the backs of their mules for the rest of the morning.

Around noon we came to a deep gorge. A bridge made of thick ropes anchored to boulders spanned the gap. Just looking at it scared me half to death.

"Do we have to use this?" I asked nervously. "Is there some other way we can cross?"

"They wouldn't have built bridges if there was another way," sighed Squint.

"Well, George doesn't like it," said Jones. "So I'd take it as a deep personal favor if you boys would look for another way. You go north, we'll go south, and we'll meet back here in an hour."

Fredo mumbled under his breath and Squint looked unhappy, but there wasn't anything they could say, and so they left.

As soon as they were out of sight, we doubled back and Jones dismounted and led his mule across the swaying bridge.

"What are you doing?" I yelled.

"Crossing the bridge. What does it look like I'm doing?" growled Jones. "And unless you want the Hardy Boys back there trying to kill us at every turn, you'll get over here too."

"But I thought they were looking for another way to cross!" I wailed.

"Will you grow up? This is the only way across," snarled Jones. "They only did what I asked to keep us from suspecting them. They haven't given up. Now quit stalling and get over here!"

With my heart in my mouth, I led my mule across the bridge. No sooner had I set foot on the other side than Jones began to hack at the ropes with his knife.

"Well, that should take care of them," said Jones as he cut the last rope. We watched as the bridge swung down and crashed against the far side of the ravine. Then, mounting our mules, we rode off down the trail.

Turn to page 82.

We joined a long line of pilgrims who were winding their way through the central courtyard of the churches.

At the head of the swaying line were high priests dressed in robes of vivid reds, blues, and purples embroidered in gold. Walking behind them were large, muscular men who shielded the priests with brightly colored gold-fringed parasols.

Horns and flutes wailed loudly, drums pounded, and sweet-smelling smoke hung heavy in the air.

"Follow me, kid," whispered Jones. As he drew even with the largest of the ancient churches, we ducked inside.

"Now what?" I asked.

"Let's check the place out," said Jones.

We checked high and low without success until Jones found a trap door behind the altar. Seizing a fat candle, we descended into the darkness that lay below.

It was creepy. The flickering candle barely lit our way through the low, narrow passage, and I kept hearing noises. Suddenly Jones stopped.

"Hold the candle," he whispered. "I'm going around the corner to take a look."

Jones crept forward and turned the corner, leaving me all alone. Then I heard him cry out in surprise.

I stood there clutching the candle, trying not to panic. What had Jones seen? Then I heard excited voices and he reappeared. With him was my father! We laughed and cried until Jones broke in.

"We can celebrate later. Why don't you tell us what's going on, Roger?"

"It's pretty simple, really. The Fascists have been following my work on the diamond laser, but they had no source of diamonds. Then they read the article on Sheba's treasure and came and got me. I was foolish to write about how diamond-rich the treasure's supposed to be, but I never thought..." My father sighed.

"You haven't told them anything, have you?" Jones asked sharply.

"Of course not," said my father. "I've given them some incorrect specifications, and it will be a while before they realize it. As for the treasure, I've got them digging trenches outside of town. There's nothing there and never has been, but they don't know that."

"Then how come you're here?" asked Jones.

"Told them I wanted to check out another site. There are a couple of guards upstairs waiting for me. They're too scared to come down and I haven't discovered another way out. But I think the treasure's down here somewhere. This area is much older than the churches. It wouldn't surprise me if Sheba used it as a burial catacomb."

"Well, what are we waiting for?" asked Jones, and off we went through the dark corridor. It twisted left and then headed down, spiraling deeper and deeper into the earth. The farther we went, the more I wondered if we'd ever get out.

I was about to suggest that we turn back when Jones found it. It didn't look like much, just a faint square outline in the ceiling. Jones picked me up and I found the latch and pushed the trap door open.

I don't think I'll ever forget my first sight of that room. Even in the candlelight it sparkled and glittered. There were casks of diamonds, rubies, emeralds, sapphires, and other precious gems. Gold and silver and ivory were piled to the ceiling.

We ran our hands through the gems, lifted the bars of silver, and gasped at the beauty of the jewelry.

"I never thought any further than this," said my father. "What do we do now?"

"Well," said Jones, "as I see it, we have two choices:

....

1. *"We can pack up some of these gems, bribe your guards, and make our escape." Turn to page 115.*

2. *"Or we can take as much as we can carry and look for another way out." Turn to page 108.*

107

"What is this place, anyhow?" I asked. "It really gives me the creeps."

"It's supposed to," said my father. "The tunnels represent hell. Pilgrims travel them in the dark, scaring themselves half to death, and emerge convinced they should be good so they can go to heaven.

"I suspect the tunnels are actually part of an earlier native religion and that the church adopted them for its own purposes."

"Do you think the priests know about the treasure?" I asked.

"I doubt it," answered my father, "or they would have removed it by now."

Just then we heard voices below us. Snuffing out the candle, Jones lifted the trap door a crack and listened. After a minute he closed it. "Pilgrims," he said.

"Excellent," said my father. "The tunnels will be crawling with them in a few minutes. It's the perfect time for us to escape. We'll just follow a bunch of them down the passage."

Working quickly, we took a few choice gold pieces and several handfuls of gemstones. Then we crouched at the trap door and waited.

Within minutes we heard voices. When they passed we slipped into the corridor and followed them.

We could hear their frightened impromptu prayers, and I must admit I shared their fear. The tunnel was creepy by candlelight, but it was terrifying in the dark.

"Jones, there's another tunnel over here on the right. I can feel it."

....

1. "Should we keep following the pilgrims and mix in with them? Maybe the guards won't notice us." Turn to page 110.

2. "Or should we take the side path? It's probably just what we've been looking for." Turn to page 112.

As we neared the end of the tunnel, Jones slipped up behind the last pilgrim and grabbed him. He gave a tiny squawk and collapsed in a dead faint.

"Probably figured the devils got him," chuckled Jones. Working quickly, he stripped the pilgrim of his robes and gave them to my dad. Then we hurried after the others.

"Pull your robes over your faces," Jones whispered as we reentered the church. And imitating the others, we bowed and nodded our way to the door.

I'll never be sure of what went wrong, but suddenly two guards jumped to their feet and drew their pistols.

"Stop!" they yelled in Italian. We burst through the door, scattering pilgrims like leaves in the wind, and ran into the thick of the crowd.

Suddenly Jones pulled out a handful of jewels and flung them up in the air. The sun danced off their facets and they fell into the crowd like brilliant rain. The crowd surged around us, shouting and scrambling for the gems.

The two guards struggled to reach us, but the excited throng would not let them pass and we slipped away like ghosts in a fog.

The trip back to the coast is something of a blur. I think half the population of Ethiopia was looking for us, but somehow we escaped.

As the powerful trimotor climbed into the sky over Africa, Jones said, "Roger, we've just made a great discovery. When this war is over, why don't the three of us come back and do this right?"

My father smiled and placed his hand on top of Jones's. Grinning like a fool, I placed my hand on top of theirs.

THE END.

We slipped into the side tunnel, and the sounds of shuffling pilgrims slowly faded away. After a few minutes Jones struck a match and lit what remained of our candle. We were in a smaller, rougher passageway.

"Probably used it to help clear out rubble," mumbled Jones. "Hope we can find a way out when we reach the end."

We reached the end soon enough. The passage ended in a blank wall with no sign of an exit. That's why I pulled the lever on the wall. I thought it would open a secret door or something.

But that's not what happened. Jones screamed "*No!*" and hurled himself at me. We crashed into the wall and there was a loud roar.

"What's that noise? What happened?" I cried in alarm.

"A Judas gate," Jones said grimly as he rolled off me and stared up at the ceiling.

"What's that?" I asked worriedly.

"A trap, kid. Put here a long time ago to catch anyone who tried to steal the treasure and escape."

"You...you mean we're trapped?"

"You got the picture, kid. Look!"

Turning, I saw my father running his hands over what appeared to be a solid wall of rubble. It filled the passage from floor to ceiling.

"Anything, Roger?"

"Nothing. Not even a crack," said my father in despair. "It's filled in solid. We're going to die."

"Not if I can help it," said Jones.

"Look here, kid. That fall cracked loose this corner of the wall. Do you see what I see?"

Putting my eye to the crack at the base of the wall, I saw daylight!

"I think this is an outer wall. No telling if we can work our way through. Even if we do, we might be stuck on the side of a mountain. But it's our only chance, and we've got to take it. You're the smallest, George, so take my knife and see what you can do."

So here I am, scraping my way through the rough volcanic rock, trying to clear a passage. Every time I move, I hear the rocks shifting above me. I'm scared. But I'm determined not to let Jones and my father down. I got us into this mess, and I'm going to dig us out of it—if it's the last thing I do!

THE END.

Using our robes, we fashioned backpacks and took a selection of some of the finer pieces. Then we stuffed handfuls of gemstones into our pockets. With one last look, we slipped through the trap door and closed it behind us.

We trudged back through the long, dark corridors until we reentered the church at last. As we stepped free of the dark walls I felt as though a great weight had been lifted from me.

Jones and I crouched in the shadows as my father called the soldiers inside and bargained with them.

At first, one of the soldiers argued against taking the bribe and I saw Jones draw his knife. But as my father added to the pile, greed replaced honor and the soldiers scooped up their treasure and hurried away.

I'd like to say it was an easy trip back, but it wasn't. We were chased by Fascists, warring tribesmen, desert bandits, and Fascists again, before we were able to board a ship for home.

As we watched the African coast disappear over the horizon, Jones and my father lifted a glass and toasted the day when we would return to the treasure of Sheba.

THE END.

SCIENCE FICTION ADVENTURE

ISAAC ASIMOV

(writing as Paul French)

THE LUCKY STARR SERIES